Text by René Gouichoux
Illustrations by Zaü
First published in France © Rue du Monde
Translation rights arranged through Hannele & Associates, Bordeaux France
Translation copyright © 2019 by Kane Press, Inc.

Publisher's Cataloging-in-Publication Data

Names: Gouichoux, René, 1950-, author. | Zaü, illustrator.
Title: Idriss and his marble / written by René Gouichoux ; illustrated by Zaü.
Description: New York, NY: Starberry Books, an imprint of Kane Press, Inc., 2019.
Summary: A young boy and his mother flee from war with lucky marble in tow.
Identifiers: LCCN 2018965798 | ISBN 978-1-63592-132-8 (Hardcover) | 978-1-63592-133-5 (ebook)
Subjects: LCSH Emigration and immigration--Juvenile fiction. | Immigrants--Juvenile fiction. | Africa--Juvenile fiction. | Refugees--Juvenile fiction. | War--Juvenile fiction. | Marbles (Game)--Juvenile fiction. | CYAC Emigration and immigration--Fiction. | Immigrants--Fiction. | Africa--Fiction. | Refugees--Fiction. | War--Fiction. | Marbles (Game)--Fiction. | BISAC JUVENILE FICTION / Social Themes / Emigration & Immigration
Classification: LCC PZ23 .G7155 I37 2019 | DDC [E]--dc23

Library of Congress Control Number: 2018965798

10 9 8 7 6 5 4 3 2 1

First published in English in the United States of America in 2019
by StarBerry Books, an imprint of Kane Press, Inc.
Printed in China

StarBerry Books is a registered trademark of Kane Press, Inc.

Book Design: Caitlin Greer

Visit us online at www.kanepress.com

Like us on Facebook
facebook.com/kanepress

Follow us on Twitter
@KanePress

IDRISS AND HIS MARBLE

Written by René Gouichoux

Illustrated by Zaü

StarBerry BOOKS

New York

Idriss has a marble.

Just one.

Every day Idriss plays on the dusty,
clay earth in front of his house.

He rolls his marble across imaginary
mountains and valleys, into caves, and
over cliffs—anything he can dream up.

It brings him happiness.

One day, Idriss hears a loud *BANG!*

His mother lifts him up with her strong arms
and carries him swiftly into the house.

Idriss hides in a corner of the kitchen.
He glimpses people of the village standing
in groups near the front door.
He hears their whispers turn to shouting.
He tells himself not to be afraid.

When the days turn calm,
Idriss brings his marble outside to play again.

But soon, the loud sounds return.

The CRACKS and BOOMS never stop.

His mother tells him it is too dangerous to play outside.

After a while, there is no one outside at all.

The people have disappeared.

His mother says they must disappear too.

On the road, his mother pulls him by the hand.
He carries nothing with him—nothing but his marble.

It's the most beautiful marble he has
ever owned—the only marble he has ever owned.

He turns one last time
to say goodbye to his home
and the dreams he had there.

For long days, Idriss and his mother walk.

They walk through the dust,
through the fear.

They ride on buses, jumping off
at the slightest sign of danger.

They continue on foot . . .

. . . until the danger passes
and another ride comes along.

They reach a huge fence.
It bristles with barbed wire,
which sparkles in the sun.

Idriss tries to see beyond this steel barrier,
but the sun stings his tired eyes.
His mother pulls him into the shadows
and tells him, "Sleep."

Idriss falls asleep, still clutching his marble.

How long has Idriss slept?
He doesn't know.

His mother shakes him awake.
She scoops him, half asleep, into her strong arms.

His mother is so graceful,
weaving their bodies beneath the barbed wire
as if she were dancing.

Idriss and his mother make haste across the beach
and approach a group of men who talk in whispers
under the shade of thick trees.

His mother joins them, shares their whispers,
passes money to the man in charge.

She turns to Idriss.
"Come! We can go."

Idriss keeps one hand in his pocket,
wrapped tightly around his marble.

Mother and son
join the crowd
who follow the man.

They make their way
to a small cove,
where an ancient
boat awaits.

Everyone runs.
They rush across the
sand and pour
into the boat
in a tangle of bodies
and voices.

Idriss runs with
them, one hand
entwined with
his mother's, the
other protecting his
marble.

When the old boat finally launches into the waves,
Idriss pulls out his marble.
He shows it to his mother and says, with a smile,
"You see, Mother? My marble brought us luck!"

His mother smiles back, but more sadly than her son.
Is it luck that she must flee her country,
the land where she grew up, where she too once played
marbles with her brothers on the clay paths?

But she smiles, despite everything.
Her son is safe. And that is lucky.

His mother strokes his hair.
"Yes, my son, your marble has brought us luck."
Idriss snuggles up against her chest.

Weighed down by the journey,
he falls asleep in her arms.

His marble, his pride,
rests safely in his hand.

A siren tears through the night, and the boat pitches back and forth.
Idriss jumps in surprise, and his marble flies into the air.
For one moment, the marble glows in a halo
of light illuminating the boat.

The blinding spotlight
comes from a mammoth
ship—the coastguard. The
marble falls into the water,
swirling and sinking into
the darkness, out of sight.

As fast as a chameleon unfolds its tongue,
a fellow traveler plunges his arm into the ocean.
He opens his fingers under the astonished eyes of Idriss.
"Here, boy, your marble!" he says.

Idriss holds out his hand to receive the marble,
which settles into place in his palm.
He beams at this traveler, this hero.

Sometime later, Idriss and his mother
have made a new home in a new land.

There, Idriss plays alone.
A child approaches. *"Want to play marbles?"* he says.

These words are new.
Idriss doesn't know them yet.

The child pours several small, colorful
glass balls from a pouch.

When Idriss sees them, he smiles.
"Marbles," the child says again.
"Marbles," Idriss repeats, understanding.

It is the first word of his new life.